AS SWEET
AS APPLE CIDER
Vermont Expressions

AS SWEET
AS APPLE CIDER
Vermont Expressions

Wolfgang Mieder

Woodcuts by Mary Azarian

The New England Press
Shelburne, Vermont

For additional copies of this book or for our catalog,
please write:

The New England Press
P.O. Box 575
Shelburne, Vermont 05482

Mieder, Wolfgang
    As sweet as apple cider : Vermont expressions / Wolfgang Mieder;
woodcuts by Mary Azarian. — 1st ed.
    p. cm.
    ISBN 0-933050-58-5 : $5.95 (pbk.)
    1. Proverbs, American—Vermont.   I. Title.
PN6426.3.V5M53 1988
398'.9'2109743—dc19   88-12464
                                                               CIP

Contents

Introduction

When the small volume of Vermont proverbs *Talk Less and Say More* appeared in 1986, the reaction by Vermonters, "flatlanders," visitors, and tourists was indeed overwhelmingly positive. The proverbs contained therein reflected at least to a certain degree some of the regional wisdom and characteristics, pointing to a rural lifestyle based on traditional Yankee independence that appears to attract many modern folk to Vermont. But proverbial wisdom is only one side of the coin as far as folk speech is concerned. In fact, while proverbs are metaphorically and often poetically expressed truths about all aspects of life, there are infinitely more colorful folk expressions that are integrated

7

into everyday speech. The latter do not express traditional wisdom, but they add metaphorical expressiveness to all types of oral and written communication. The present collection of such proverbial expressions is, therefore, intended to be a companion to the earlier book on Vermont proverbs. Together both books mirror the rich traditional folk speech of the inhabitants of the state of Vermont.

A basic definition of a *proverb* declares that it is a concise statement of an apparent truth that has currency among certain people. Proverbs are thus thoughts expressed in complete sentences. Some poignant Vermont examples would be "You can't sell the cow and have the milk too," "Dunghills rise and castles fall," and "Every cider apple has a worm," among others. In contrast, *proverbial expressions* do not contain wisdom that is handed down from generation to generation. They are mere metaphorical statements that have gained currency because of their striking and colorful images. Instead of being complete sentences and thoughts, they are only partial phrases and take on actual meaning only after having been integrated into a particular speech act. Such Vermont proverbial expressions as "To search for a mouse in a straw stack," "To be too old a bird to learn a new tune," and "To swallow the cow and get stuck on the tail" all need a grammatical subject, a conjugated verb, and a context in order to take on a meaningful function. Nevertheless, they belong to our ready-made formulaic speech patterns on which people draw freely when they wish or need to express themselves in a metaphorical fashion.

In addition to proverbs and proverbial expressions, there are several subgenres that belong to the proverbial stock of every language. Of particular interest are the so-called *proverbial comparisons*, which might once again be subdivided into three classes. There are first of all those similes using the conjunction *as* — for example, "As busy as a fiddler's elbow," "As crooked as a snake in a hurry," and "As cold as a hot-water bag in the morning." The second group is made up of similes employing the conjunction *like*, for example "Shaped like an old appletree" and "To feel like a skunk in hell with its back broken." Finally, there are many proverbial comparisons that follow the structure of an adjective in the comparative degree followed by *than*, as can be seen in such examples as "No bigger than a pint of cider half drunk up," "Longer than a wet week," "Hotter than love in haying time," and the like. Indeed, since proverbial comparisons with these structures are particularly frequent, this book includes three special chapters of them with numerous colorful texts. Many others are, of course, interspersed in all the other chapters as well.

One further subgenre of proverbial expressions deserves mentioning. Folklorists often speak of *proverbial exaggerations*, which may be defined as traditional formulas used to describe the extraordinary degree to which someone or something performs a particular action or possesses a certain characteristic. Many of these exaggerations are based on the structural formula *so . . . (that)*, clearly illustrated in such texts as "She is so thin you have to shake the sheets to find her," "He is so narrowminded that he can see through a keyhole with both eyes," and "It rained so hard that the water stood ten feet out of the well." But there are also plenty of metaphorical exaggerations that follow no particular pattern. All of them are obvious humorous or satirical indications that folk speech reflects the predilection of the common people to couch their expressive language into formulaic statements based on the most vivid images.

As far as this collection of Vermont expressions of various types is concerned, it should be noted that only texts are included that have been recorded in the state of Vermont. This does not mean that some of the expressions might not be known in neighboring states like Maine, New Hampshire, and New York. However, a conscious attempt has usually been made to exclude expressions that are known more or less throughout the United States. Such texts as "To make ends meet," "To put the cart before the horse," "As hard as a rock," and "To cast pearls before swine," do not appear. Some proverbial expressions are so ancient and internationally disseminated through translations of the classics and the Bible that they have become part of a basic phraseology that permits metaphorical communication to take place among members of different cultures.

What this book contains is a regional collection of proverbial expressions assembled from oral and written sources in Vermont. To ascertain whether a particular expression is indigenous only to Vermont would be extremely difficult and in most cases impossible. What is of importance is that the texts are current in Vermont and that they mirror a certain local flavor. For example, instead of the more generally known expression "Not to know someone from a hole in the ground," this book registers the rurally oriented parallel texts "Not to know someone from a bale of hay" and "Not to know someone from a cord of wood." The same phenomenon can be observed by the juxtaposition of the common expression "To cut off one's nose to spite one's face" and the Vermontish "To burn a barn to kill the rats." Notice also such pairs as "To be tickled pink" and "To be tickled spitless," "That's the way the ball bounces" and "That's the way the cat jumps," and "Hotter than hell" and "Hotter than hell's back-kitchen." The national proverbial stock appears bland and colorless due to overuse, and some expressions deserve to be labeled with the negative term of *cliché*. On the other hand, the regional folk expressions of Vermont are refreshingly unique in their metaphors, meanings, humor, and satire. Many of them are clearly crude, obnoxious, unflattering, malevolent, and aggressively blunt. They serve people as a linguistic tool to vent their feelings and frustrations. All these proverbial expressions show that the real Vermonter and those who make Vermont their home and who try to be part of this lifestyle do not shy away from "calling a spade a spade."

The sources of the over five hundred texts put together in this collection are too numerous to list here individually. Many of them were collected in oral use over the past nearly two decades. Others were located in the literary works of such Vermont authors as Rowland E. Robinson, Dorothy Canfield Fisher, Allen R. Foley, Walter Hard, and others. All issues of the two Vermont folklore journals, the *Green Mountain Whittlin's* and *The Potash Kettle*, were painstakingly checked for texts. I feel indebted to all the contributors to these treasure chests of Vermont folklore, but I also owe much gratitude and credit to the work of two former English professors at the University of Vermont, Muriel Hughes and Leon Dean, on Vermont proverbs prior to my own collecting activities.

As was stated above, I see this small book as a pendant to my earlier book on Vermont proverbs. Once again, the rich materials have been divided into small chapters on many different subjects. There are also three chapters that reflect the predominant linguistic structures of the numerous proverbial comparisons. It would have been impossible to place some of them into the other fifteen chapters since the texts only come to life (i.e., gain actual meaning) when placed into a speech context. Both books together have now registered about one thousand proverbs and proverbial expressions current in Vermont. It is my hope that I have found a representative sample of "Vermont proverbiality." But please, let me hear from you if you have proverbs or proverbial expressions that should be added to my archive. We all use these traditional gems! All it takes is to listen to and to become aware of the proverbial speech that epitomizes the spirit of Vermonters.

So frail as to be blown away . . .

CARES
AND
DILEMMAS

Up the creek without a paddle.

He feels as neglected as the bones
at a banquet.

I don't care if it costs every
cow in the barn.

To be buried under shavings.
[To be lost in detail.]

As worried as a toad under a harrow.

As hopeful as an old maid looking
under the bed.

To feel like two cents.

Like dragging a cat out from
under a barn.

So tough you couldn't stick your
fork in the gravy.

Worse than eating bread and milk out
of a jug with a knitting needle.

She doesn't give a straw.

So frail as to be blown away
by the next breeze.

I'm enjoying poor health.

Not care a feather.

It took the tuck right out of me.

As brittle as glass.

You don't weigh more than a straw hat.
[Said to an insignificant person.]

To be laid up for repairs.
[To recover from illness.]

They don't care a button for hunting.

It's not to be sneezed at by people
with no noses.

She doesn't feel like setting
the river afire.

It doesn't make a straw's difference.

She can hardly spin a thread.
[She is not feeling well.]

To burn a barn to kill the rats.

To be as deep in the mud [dirt] as
another is in the mire.

He got into a puckersnatch.
[He got into a tight corner.]

I didn't get my seed back.
[I had poor results.]

Not care a pin's head.

Like a cow chasing a hare.

No bigger than a pint of cider
half drunk up.

A hole so big you could drive
a truck through it.

To feel like a skunk in hell with
its back broken.

They have more kids than a flight
of stairs.

He'd skin a mouse...

MONEY
AND
THRIFTINESS

He'd skin a mouse for its
hide and tallow.

To make the strap and the buckle meet.

He is so tight, his eyelids squeak
when he winks.

Can't afford hay for a nightmare.

To set oneself up in a butter tub.
[To marry a rich woman.]

As poor as a parson's cat.

A ten-dollar hat on a ten-cent head.

Money comes from him like
drops of blood.

To save at the spigot and lose
at the bunghole.

Some people will cry poor on
a full stomach.

He would pinch a penny until
it squeaked.

This is way up in the picture.
[This is too expensive.]

He motions to money, and it
rolls his way.

To have a champagne taste and
a beer pocketbook.

It costs more than it comes to.

She'd skin a woodchuck to save a cent.

To make money like hay.

This is about as paying a job as
whitewashing rat manure and
selling it for rice.

He would skin a louse and send the
hide and fat to market.

To squeeze a dollar until
the eagle squeals.

His wallet shuts too tight.

Money slips through her fingers like
water running over the dam.

To save a cent by wasting a dollar.

As free from money as a frog
is of feathers.

He ain't got a pot to wet in nor
a window to throw it out of.

A cow with snowshoes...

BEAUTY
AND
HOMELINESS

She's as dainty as a cow with
snowshoes on.

As homely as a hedge fence.

You look as though you've been
dragged through a brush heap.

As cute as a little red wagon
all painted red.

Shaped like an old appletree.

As plump as a partridge.

Built like a bull heifer.

As homely as the north end of
a mule going south.

He's so thin, he has to stand twice in
the same place to make a good shadow.

As bald as an apple.

She waddles like a hurried duck.

To have eyes that look like two holes
in a blanket.

As handsome as a dollar.

Homely enough to stop a freight train.

He is as fat as a woodchuck.

You have a nose so big, you could
bust pumpkins on it.

That dress looks as if the cloth had
been hung on the line and struck
out by lightning.

He's homely enough to suck eggs.

It is about as pretty as last year's
bird's nest.

As ugly as a mud fence.

You look as though you were dead
and had been dug up again.

As plain as a pipestem.

Blushing like a June rose.

She looks like she was drawn through
a knothole.

As homely as hell is wicked.

Her head looks as if it had worn
out two bodies.

She is so thin, you have to shake
the sheets to find her.

You've got eyes like a potato and
ears like a cabbage.

As busy as a fiddler's elbow.

BUSYNESS
— AND —
LAZINESS

As lazy as a toad at the bottom
of a well.

He is as busy as a bumblebee in hell.

They're going at it like a bull
at the gate.

You're as lazy as a hound in
'possum season.

As busy as a one-armed man
with the hives.

She is as busy as a one-eyed cat
watching two rat holes.

25

He works with one eye on the clock.

As busy as a fiddler's elbow.

To putter around all day in
a peck measure.
[To waste time by working slowly.]

He's too lazy to ache when
he's in pain.

To be as busy as a hen with one chick.

She never rides the day she saddles.
[She is lazy.]

To bust one's boiler.
[To work too hard.]

Busier than a bird dog on
a cement walk.

We are going at it full chisel.

As busy as a cow's tail in fly time.

She'll stick to it like teazles.

As busy as a one-armed paper-hanger
with the seven-year itch.

As industrious as a beaver.

She's as busy as a toad in a puddle.

We worked all day in half a bushel.
[We accomplished very little.]

As busy as a bee in a tar barrel.

To start in the middle and end
at both ends.
[To get nowhere.]

He's as lazy as a turtle nine days
after it's been killed.

As busy as an old hen with a brood of
ducklings at a millpond.

CHARACTER
— AND —
VALUE

You're so low, you'd have to stand on
stilts to scratch a snake's back.

A big frog in a little puddle.

That doesn't amount to buy dust.

As independent as a man on the town.

Not worth a rye straw.

I feel like crawling through
a knothole and pulling the knot
in after me.
[I feel worthless.]

No better than sour apples.

A wagonload of postholes.
[Nothing.]

That doesn't amount to any more than
the figure 9 with the tail cut off.

If he fell into a well, he would come
out with a gold watch and a chain.

As cheap as dirt.

He ain't worth a tinker's damn.

He thinks he's the whole team and the
little dog under the wagon.

As big as ten cents' worth of
dandelion greens.

That will never be noticed on
a trotting horse.
[That's too insignificant.]

As independent as a hog on ice.

That doesn't amount to sugar
on a stick.

He's so narrow minded, he can look
through a keyhole with both
eyes at once.

Not worth the north wind in
a rabbit's track.

Pretty small potatoes and few
in a hill.

She thinks the sun rises and
sets on her.

Not worth a fly wing.

Rolling off a log . . .

COMPARISONS
—— WITH ——
THAN

Homelier than a basket of knotholes.

Darker than the rear end of midnight.

No bigger than a fly's ear.

Thicker than two hands in a mitten.

Longer than a freight train.

Slicker than a trout's ear.

Tighter than the shingles on a roof.

Easier than rolling off
a log backward.

Tougher than old hickory.

Busier than four hounds on one scent.

Noisier than a threshing machine.

Happier than a pig in a puddle of mud.

Darker than a black cow's belly.

Smaller than the point of a needle.

Drunker than a bumble bee.

Higher than a fairground fence.

Deader than hay.

Lower than a snake's belly.

Louder than a harvest thunderstorm.

Bigger than Mt. Mansfield.

Longer than a brook.

Slicker than goose grease.

Darker than a stack of black cats
with their eyes put out.

Tighter than the bark to a tree.

Finer than a hummingbird's pinfeather.

Colder than a dog's nose.

Tougher than green elm.

SPEED
AND
INERTIA

So slow, you can watch the
snails whiz by.

As quick as a hopping grasshopper
with its tail on fire.

Behind like a cow's tail.

Slower than cold molasses running
uphill in the wintertime.

As quick as a steel trap.

Slow as turtles.

Faster than a toad lapping lightning.

To go like a scared jackrabbit.

He's so slow, he'll rot in his tracks.

Quicker than you can get off
a wet shirt.

Slower than the hind wheels of time
greased with cold molasses.

Faster than a boy killing snakes.

As slow as a hog on ice with its
tail frozen in.

He went out of there like hell
beating tan bark.

Slower than the growth of grindstone.

He's so slow, he's afraid that if he
moves, he'll get going and can't stop.

In two shakes of a lamb's tail.
[In a short time.]

To creep like a snail.

Quicker than hell ever scorched
a feather.

As slow as molasses in January.

To walk and talk like hens in harvest.

Slower than death on crutches.

Like a pig's tail—going all day
and nothing done at night.

Faster than a hen can pick up corn.

Slower than the growth of
a dead hemlock.

Quicker than chain lightning.

She ran as fast as pudding
would creep.

Talking to a post.

SPEECH
AND
SILENCE

He shut up like a mousetrap.

As loud as a watermill.

She talked as though her tongue were
hung in the middle and wagged
at both ends.

As quiet as a millpond.

As silent as a midnight minute.

He talks the handle off the pump.

As silently as a snail slips over
a cabbage leaf on a dewy morning.

She babbles like a brook.

To talk a living storm.

As speechless as cats in
cloudy weather.

He was born with a long tongue.
[He is a big talker.]

To go off and leave one's
mouth talking.
[To talk too much.]

Mouth enough for two sets
of false teeth.

You might as well talk to a post.

To yell like a pig under a gate.

She can talk a tin ear off a donkey.

Clucking like a hen bringing
home her brood.

He's a regular threshing machine.
[He talks too much and too loud.]

To talk the tin ear off an iron dog.

Put your tongue between your teeth
and try to wiggle your ears.
[Don't gossip.]

His pond has run out.
[He has finished talking.]

A tongue hung in the middle and
sharp on both ends.

To mutter in one's beard.

You might as well paint it on
the fence as tell her.
[She tells everything anyway.]

As quiet as a lighting of a fly on
a feather-duster.

Freeze your tongue and give your
teeth a sleighride.
[Be silent.]

Water in the shoes. . .

EXPENDABILITY
AND
INABILITY

To search for a mouse in
a straw stack.

As clumsy as a cow with its foot
stuck in the mud.

She doesn't need it any more than she
needs water in her shoes.

He couldn't hit a meeting house
standing still.

As helpless as a man on
a milking stool.

He is as handy as a hog with a fiddle.

She can't spin a thread.
[She is incapable.]

He doesn't need it any more than a
toad needs a watch.

To throw snowballs into hell to put
out the fire.

You don't need it any more than you
need a pocket in your undershirt.

He stumbled around like a blind horse
in a pumpkin patch.

As useless as a Christmas tree on
New Year's Eve.

They don't need this any more than
a hen needs teeth.

That fits like a shirt on a beanpole.

As unhandy as a hoopskirt.

A whole lot of milking but
only one cow.

As useless as twenty tailors
around a buttonhole.

This fits like a bearskin
on a woodchuck.

As useful as a pothole in the rain.

He doesn't need it any more than
a pig needs a wallet.

We don't need this any more than a pig
needs a toothbrush.

As useless as wet powder.

She has as little use for this as
a hog has for a white collar.

As handy as a cow with a gun.

As helpless as a baby.

This is of no more use than a spare
pump in a corn crib.

Fits like a saddle on a sow.

He doesn't need it any more than
a cow needs two tails.

Throwing a bull by the tail.

VIRTUE
— AND —
VICE

She was pure as snow, but she drifted.

As crooked as a snake in a hurry.

I wouldn't trust him any farther than
I can throw a bull by the tail.

She is so prim and proper, butter
wouldn't melt in her mouth.

He's as crooked as a cow's horn.

He'd steal the saddle off a nightmare.

He is as straight as a yard
of pump-water.

As crooked as a dog's hind leg.

She is as chaste as snow.

As loose as a fiddle string.

She doesn't wear enough clothes to
make a veil for a hummingbird.

He's so crooked, he could hide
behind a corkscrew.

As prim as an old maid.

To take someone for a sleighride.
[To deceive someone.]

As square as a block of granite.

He was so crooked, he couldn't
stand up straight.

He has three hands—a right hand,
a left hand, and a little behind hand.

As straight as a lamb's hind leg.

Crookeder than a ram's horn.

As crooked as a country road.

I wouldn't trust him to feed
garbage to a pig.

To milk the town dry.
[To cheat, to exploit.]

He is too crooked to lie
straight in bed.

As two-faced as a double-bitted ax.

I wouldn't trust him as far as I
could throw this house by the chimney.

As crooked as a furrow.

She is as loose as ashes and
twice as dirty.

He's so crooked, they'll have to use
a corkscrew to bury him.

As chaste as an icicle.

Doesn't know enough to pull in his head . . .

IGNORANCE
— AND —
STUPIDITY

He could get lost in his own
sap orchard.

You don't know beef from broomstick.

He hasn't the brains God gave an owl.

I wouldn't know him if I met him in
a cup of tea.

As stupid as a woodchuck.

He doesn't know enough to be
assistant janitor to a corn crib.

As dumb as a stone wall.

She can't tell a pumpkin from a hole
in the ground.

She doesn't know him from
a bale of hay.

As free of brains as a frog is
free of feathers.

You're so stupid, you couldn't find
your way out of a wet paper bag.

What she doesn't know would make
a big book.

As wise as a wisdom tooth.

He doesn't know enough to pour water
out of a boot with the directions
written on the heel.

You are bright enough to be an idiot.

To have a dearth of corn in the attic.
[To lack brains.]

He doesn't know enough to ache
when he's in pain.

She is so dumb, she couldn't crawl
through a knothole backward.

47

You don't know enough to suck
alum and drool.

I wouldn't know him from last
year's bird's nest.

He's as big a fool as Johnnie's hound
that swam four miles upstream to get
a drink of water.

He lost his mind, and he doesn't seem
to miss it.

He never knew nothing and forgot
the nothing he never knew.

To act like a turkey and think
like a groundhog.

He hasn't got a brain in his body
nor any place to put one.

He don't know nothing and always will.

She doesn't know enough to boil water.

He can't see a hole through a ladder.

Dumb as a doorknob.

His brain jelled a long time ago.

We don't know her from a cord of wood.

He didn't scarcely know which end
his head was on.

She has no more sense than to put
a milk bucket under a bull.

He doesn't know enough to pull in
his head when he shuts the window.

Your brain is so small, it would
rattle in a thimble.

He doesn't know enough to
blow hot soup.

She is so stupid that she can't boil
water without burning it.

He doesn't know twice around
a hoe handle.

She was behind the door when the
brains were passed out.

As stupid as a bag of hammers.

He hasn't enough sense to pound sand
in a rat hole.

To grow like grass in May.

COMPARISONS
WITH
LIKE

To stare like a mad bull.

He stands out like a blackberry
in a pan of milk.

To grin like a toad chewing lightning.

To stick like a puppy to a bone.

He argues like a jug-handle—
all on one side.

It stinks like a poisoned rat.

That kiss sounded like a cow pulling
her foot out of the mud.

He hammered like a woodpecker.

To grow like grass in May.

She jumped around like a flea
in a mitten.

To look like a hen in a windstorm.

To cling like a wet kitten to
a hot brick.

You stick out like a wart on
an old maid's nose.

To hop like a pea on a hot griddle.

To squeak like a sled runner on
a frosty morning.

To shine like a good deed in
a naughty world.

She jumped like a cat out
of a woodbox.

He looks like the last run of shad.

He's quiet like a tree without
a leaf stirring.

To die like a cornered rat.

To stick like bees to honey.

This looks like something
the dog dragged in.

To fit like a duck's foot in the mud.

To mill around like a herd of cows.

It squeaks and grunts just like
a litter of hungry pigs.

To jump like a trout.

You look like a drowned mouse.

To swallow the cow...

ACTIONS
AND
HABITS

We're swinging on the same gate.
[We are agreeing.]

To be plastered to the ears.

To swallow the cow and get stuck
on the tail.

He wants to sell the bearskin before
the bear is caught.

To act as if one had been brought
up in a barn.

To butt one's head against
a stone wall.

I don't feel like jumping over
a five-rail fence.
[I don't feel too energetic.]

To break the logjam.

Spit on the floor and be sociable.

That's the way the cat jumps.

I could eat a horse and chase
its rider.

His wishbone is stronger
than his backbone.

To get one's religion fixed.
[To attend church.]

You would take a worm from
a blind hen's mouth.

Draw in one's horns.
[Retreat.]

I'll hit you so hard, you'll starve
to death bouncing.

He has all his taste in his mouth.
[He is a crude person.]

She's so nosy, she can hear
the grass grow.

We're always climbing up fool's hill.
[We're learning by experience.]

He acts like he was raised
in a sawmill.
[He leaves the door open in
cold weather.]

To handle without mittens.
[To handle roughly.]

I'll have to wear that dress from
mill to meeting.
[It will have to do for all occasions.]

If your foresight was as good as
your hindsight, you'd see better by
a damn sight.

You don't have spunk enough to break
up a setting hen.

Moss grows on his head...

AGE
AND
TIME

Many an applecart will tip
over before then.

As long as a day without bread.

To be wise before one's time.

She's trying to be a cowslip
blooming in September.
[She tries to hide her age.]

As old as my tongue, and little older
than my teeth.

That horse is old enough to have been
born in Adam's stable.

To have to wait until the cows
come home.
[To wait for a long time.]

As long as grass grows and water runs.

When you were a pile of sawdust,
and I was a little shaving.
[A long time ago.]

Short and sweet, like
a donkey's gallop.

Like old boots, past all
hope of mending.

It'll be a long day and a dark night
before you see him again.

To be happy by the month.

He is so old, moss is growing on
his bald head.

To expand and contract like an
old woman's conscience.

She looks as ancient as the hills.

Longer than a wet week.

When ice is hot.
[Never.]

To be too old a bird to learn
a new tune.

Older than the devil's grandfather.

When robins wear overalls.
[Never.]

Like a young bear with all his
troubles before him.

It will last about as long as
a snowball in June.

MOODS
AND
TEMPERS

As mean as a horse-blanket thief on
a cold winter day.

She was tickled spitless.

He'd sour milk by looking at it.

As nervous as a cat watching a mouse.

He's sorry from his boots up.

As short as piecrust.

A temper like a meat ax.

As proud as a pig with two tails.

She gave him a combing out.
[She scolded him.]

He's a tough cud for somebody to chew.

As cranky as an old maid.

Livelier than a young heifer.

He is all lathered up.
[He is excited.]

As calm as a clock.

Crosser than a bear with a sore head.

She's as snappy as a steel trap.

He's so mad, he's chewing nails
and spitting rust.

As chipper as a chipmunk.

He is so mean, he stinks.

To take the bit in one's teeth.
[To take control.]

He pretty near jumped out
of his shoes.

As nervous as a cat with wet feet.

She snapped her whip.
[She lost her temper.]

As jumpy as a hen on a hot brick.

Angry enough to bite a shingle
nail in two.

To kick over the traces.
[To get out of hand.]

As cool as a cucumber.

As anxious as a brooding hen.

As nasty as hogs.

She is so cross-looking, she must
have been weaned on a sour pickle.

Colder than blue blazes.

HOT
AND
COLD

Hotter than love in haying time.

As cold as a barn.

To sweat so much, one can feel little
fishes swimming up and down.

Cold enough to freeze the hair of
a dog's back.

As warm as wool.

Colder than a dead puppy's nose.

To have no more warmth
than an iceberg.

As hot as toast.

It's cold enough to freeze
the ears off a donkey.

Hotter than hell's back-kitchen.

As cold as a frog.

He didn't know enough to hunt shade
on a hot day.

As cold as a corn crib.

As warm as a mouse in a churn.

Colder than a dead lamb's tongue.

Today is hotter than a puppies' nest.

As cold as a stone.

Sweating like a man mowing.

It's colder than all get out.

Hotter than frying doughnuts
in sizzling fat.

Colder than blue blazes.

I am sweating like a pitcher with
ice-water in it.

As hot as horse piss.

It's colder than charity.

Hot as the hinges of hell.

Colder than ice.

It's cold enough to freeze a brass
monkey's tail off.

Hotter than love in July.

As cold as a hot-water bag
in the morning.

WEATHER
— AND —
SEASONS

The only people who predict weather around here are fools and strangers.

We have had hardly enough rain to drown a flea.

As mild as the spring.

As dry as a chip.

It rained so hard that the water stood ten feet out of the well.

She's got spring fever.

As welcome as snow in harvest.

The bluejays are hollering for
cold and snow.

As uncertain as the weather.

Coming out like frogs after
a heavy rain.

It will go like dew before the sun.

Drier than a covered bridge.

As wet as a drowned rat.

To sell like green peas in spring.

It's no haying day.

As bare as the trees in winter.

It was so dry that the fish kicked up
an awful dust getting upstream.

As certain as the sun is rising.

It glistened like the cold stars of
a winter's night.

Poor man's manure.
[Snow.]

Raining like suds.

As loud as thunder.

As merry as a cricket in autumn.

It's a good sap day.

As fickle as the weathercock.

The winter's back is broken.

As fresh as flowers in spring.

Melting away like snow before the sun.

As calm as dew.

We always get a January thaw, even if it doesn't come until March.

A skunk at a lawn party . . .

COMPARISONS
WITH
AS

As rare as a three-legged calf.

As green as a grasshopper.

As black as chimney soot.

As dull as ditchwater.

As prickly as a hedgehog.

As slick as a hot knife
through butter.

As maggotty as old cheese.

As hard as a millstone.

As glum as a toad.

As sure as hell is a mousetrap.

As deep as a well.

As fat as pork.

As red as a spanked baby.

As full as a tick.

As high as the steam from a heap
of warm horse doughnuts on
a frosty morning.

As round as an apple.

As tough as a knot [of a tree].

As likely as water running uphill.

As white as marble.

As pleased as a cat with two tails.

As dead as a hammer.

As happy as a bumblebee in
a field of clover.

As sweet as syrup.

As popular as a skunk at a lawn party.

As rotten as an old stump.

As shy as a colt.

As black as a crow's wing.

As slippery as a greased pig.

As snug as a flea in a blanket.

As empty as last year's bird's nest.

As tough as bull beef at
a penny a pound.

As soft as a colt's nose.

As gray as inside a pewter dish.

As blind as a post.

As odd as a fifth wheel to a coach.

As sour as buttermilk.

As thick as wool.

As subtle as a brick through
a glass window.

As scarce as hen teeth.

As hot as an old radish.

As sweet as apple cider.

As white as falling snow.

As hard as dragging a cat out from
under the barn.

As nimble as a doe.

As green as a gourd.

As tickled as a child with
a little red wagon.

As welcome as a snowball in June.

As blue as forget-me-nots.

As good as the rest, but not the best.

As happy as a skunk in a hen roost.

As red as a tomato.

As dead as a log.

As strong as a moose.

As dull as a hoe.

As black as a stack of black cats
in the dark.

As big as life and twice as natural.

8597   5989